A GIFT FOR:

FROM:

All DC characters and elements
© & ™ DC Comics. (s18)

Hallmark

Published in 2018 by Hallmark Gift Books,
a division of Hallmark Cards, Inc.,
Kansas City, MO 64141
Visit us on the Web at Hallmark.com.

Editorial Director: Delia Berrigan
Editor: Kara Goodier
Art Director: Chris Opheim
Designer: Scott Swanson
Production Designer: Dan Horton

Writers: Andrew Blackburn, Alex Boney,
Kevin Dilmore, Jake Gahr, and Kat Hollyer
Illustrated by Kelly Green

ISBN: 978-1-63059-767-2
BOK1099

Made in China
0118

DAD MAY LOOK LIKE A

REGULAR GUY

ON THE OUTSIDE, BUT WE ALL

KNOW THE TRUTH—HE'S A

SUPER

HERO.

HE'S ALWAYS THERE WHEN RUBBER MEETS THE ROAD.

CK BACK, STRETCH OUT, AND RELAX.

WHEN I NEED HIM,
HE'S THERE

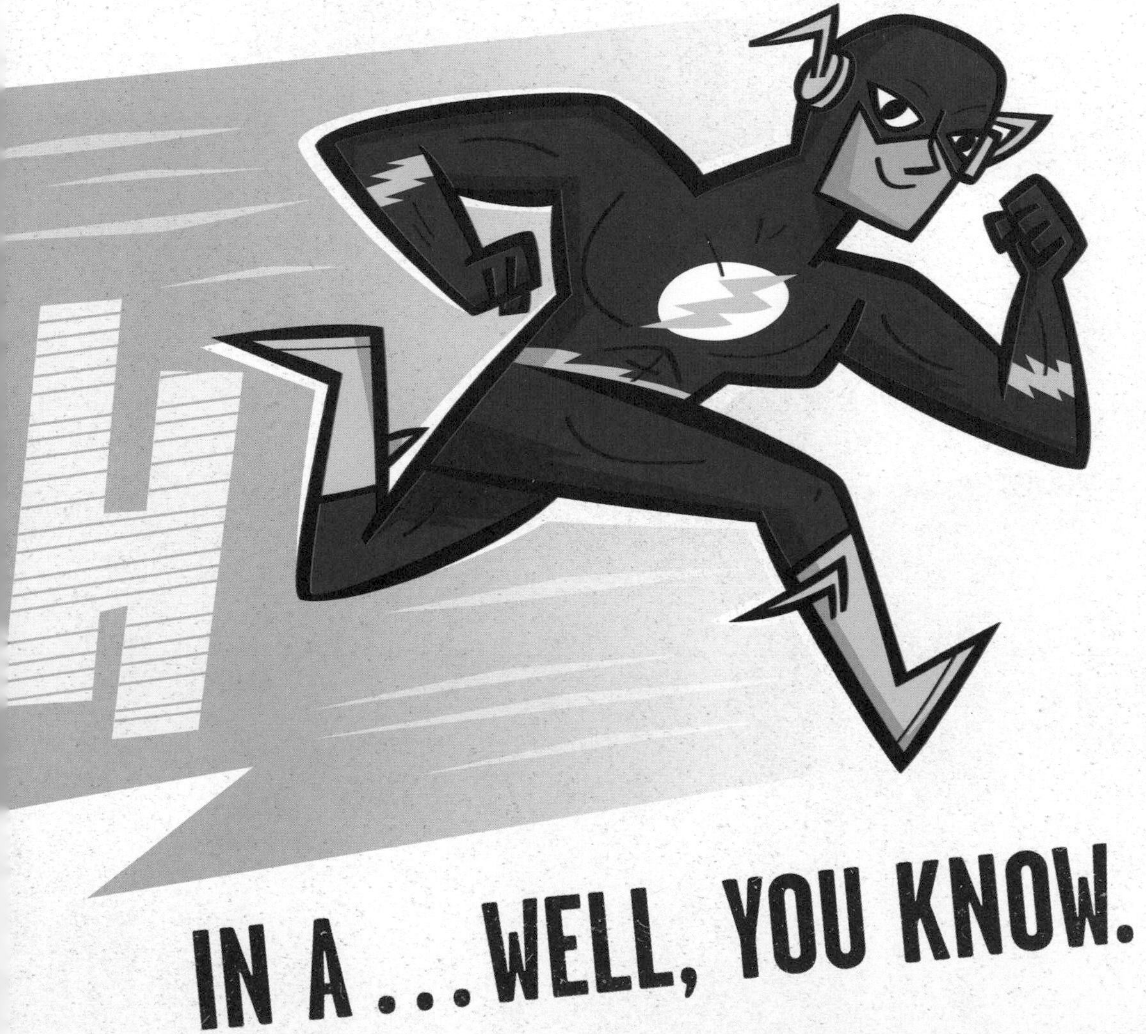

IN A . . . WELL, YOU KNOW.

DAD REMINDS ME THAT I'M STRONGER THAN I THINK I AM.

HE TAUGHT ME
THAT BEING
A JOKER
CAN BE A
GOOD THING.
SOMETIMES.

DAD MAKES THE FUN APPEAR OUT OF NOWHERE.

WHEN LIFE
SENDS ME INTO
CHOPPY WATERS,
HE HELPS ME
GET THROUGH
THEM.

DAD ALWAYS COMES THROUGH FOR ME...

...EVEN WHEN HE'S JUST WINGIN' IT.

HE TEACHES ME TO BELIEVE IN MYSELF, NO MATTER WHO OR WHAT I'M UP AGAINST.

DAD KNOWS WHEN TO KEEP HIS COOL.

THERE'S NOTHING SMALL ABOUT HIS AWESOMENESS...

...BECAUSE HE ALWAYS SHOWS UP BIG WHEN I NEED HIM.

HIS ADVICE IS RIGHT ON TARGET.

DAD TRUSTS YOU TO BE RESPONSIBLE, EVEN WITH THE IMPORTANT STUFF.

HE KNOWS HOW TO GO WITH THE FLOW.

DAD MAKES SURE I HAVE EVERYTHING I NEED.

HE ALWAYS
HAS THE
RIGHT TOOLS
FOR THE JOB.

WHEN I NEED TO TALK, HE'S ALWAYS READY TO LISTEN.

IT SEEMS LIKE NOTHING CAN STUMP HIM.

DAD KNOWS THAT HAVING A BIG IMAGINATION CAN BE A GOOD THING.

EVEN AT HIS BUSIEST, HE KNOWS HOW IMPORTANT IT IS TO TAKE IT SLOW.

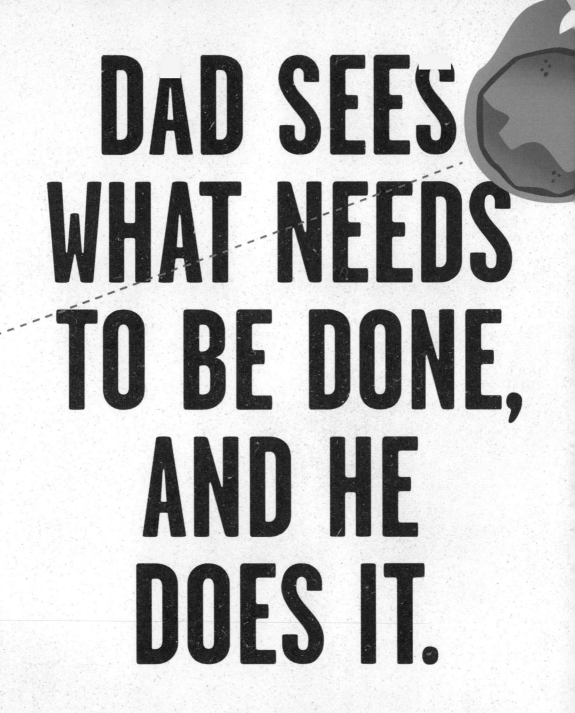

DAD SEES WHAT NEEDS TO BE DONE, AND HE DOES IT.

HE GIVES A WHOLE NEW MEANING TO "MR. FIX-IT."

HE ENCOURAGES ME TO AIM HIGH IN EVERYTHING I DO.

WATCHING HIM MAKES ME WANT TO PURSUE MY PASSIONS, TOO.

DAD CAN SEE RIGHT THROUGH ANY EXCUSE.

WHEN THINGS GET TOUGH, HE ALWAYS HELPS ME KEEP MY HEAD ABOVE WATER.

MOST HEROES HAVE A WEAKNESS, BUT THAT'S JUST ONE WAY HE'S MORE THAN THE AVERAGE HERO.

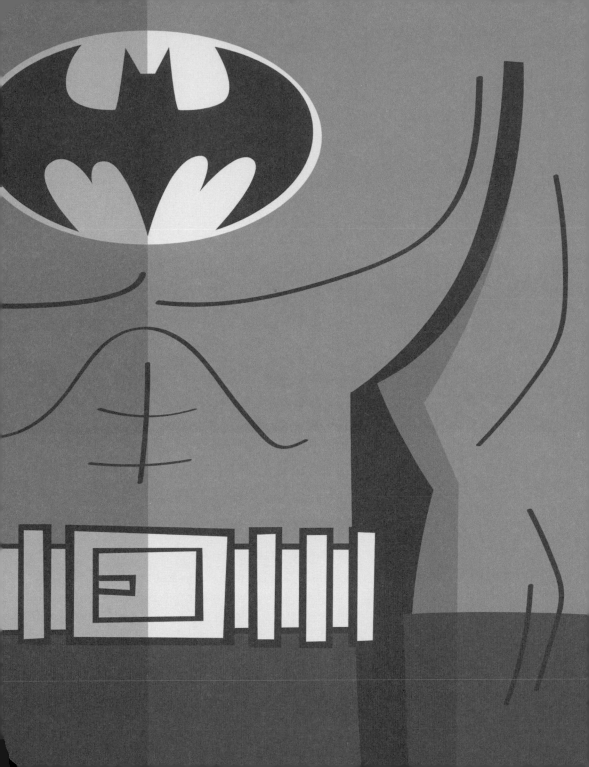

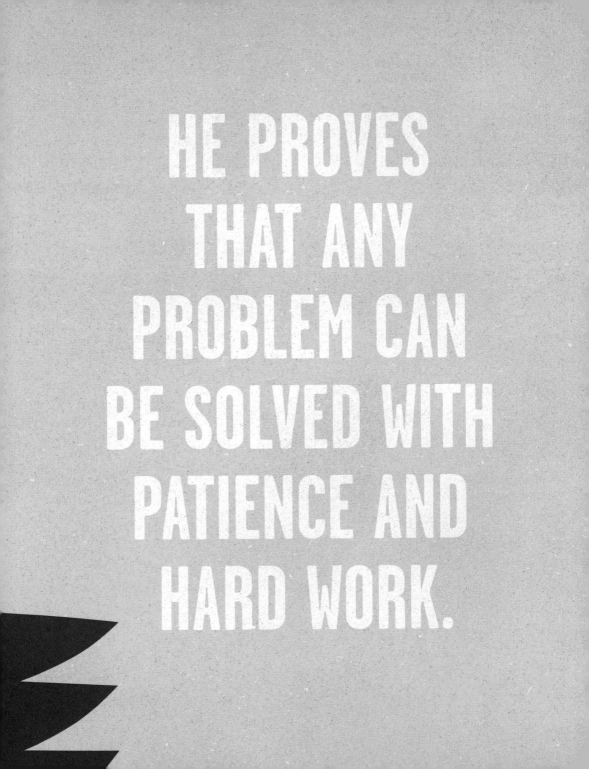

HE PROVES
THAT ANY
PROBLEM CAN
BE SOLVED WITH
PATIENCE AND
HARD WORK.

HE CAN WEATHER ANY STORM...AND PROTECT HIS FAMILY FROM IT, TOO.

DAD HELPS ME NOT GET STUCK IN THE WHIRLWIND OF LIFE.

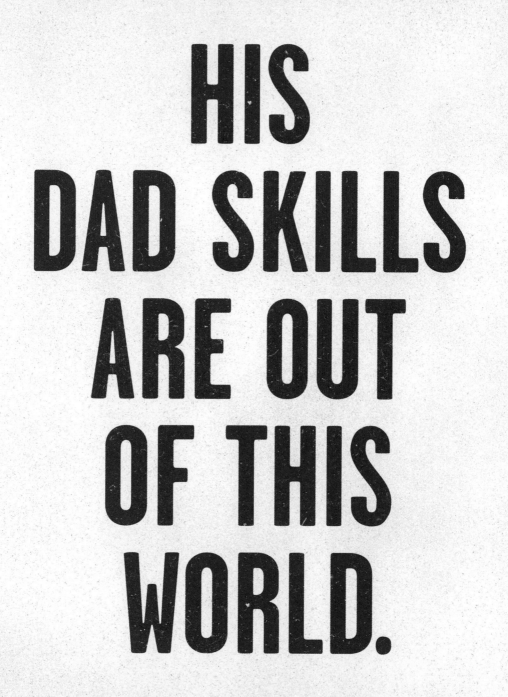

HIS
DAD SKILLS
ARE OUT
OF THIS
WORLD.

HE ALWAYS COMES THROUGH IN A PINCH.

AND HE'S NOT
JUST A HERO
TO ME, HE'S A
HERO
TO EVERYONE.

If you enjoyed this book
or it has touched your life in some way,
we'd love to hear from you.

Please write a review at Hallmark.com,
e-mail us at booknotes@hallmark.com,
or send your comments to:

Hallmark Book Feedback
P.O. Box 419034
Mail Drop 100
Kansas City, MO
64141